My Melbourne Adventure
Belongs to:

Oliv'n Keenan

I love you

Look out for Nelly The Wombat
.....she likes to hide!

For Harry and for Patrick and Hamish

Thanks to family and friends for your continued support.

Harry loves 'writing' letters to his Grandparents known as Mac and Pa.
'My Melbourne Adventure' is another letter Harry wishes to
share with you as part of the 'My Adventure Series'.

This series has been created to promote Australia.
More important however, it is to encourage children to have a sense of fun and imagination.
We also hope that children will be encouraged to write a letter….and post it!

Look out for further books in this series:
My Aussie Bush Adventure
My Phillip Island Adventure
My Warburton Adventure
My Mornington Peninsula Adventure
My Sydney Adventure
My Tassie Adventure

Published by Rothwell Publishing
9 Clarke Avenue Warburton, Victoria, Australia, 3799
www.rothwellpublishing.com
rothwellpublishing@bigpond.com
Tele: 61 3 5966 5628

First Published 2005
Reprinted 2006 twice
Text copyright © Jo Rothwell 2005
Illustrations copyright © Bryce Rothwell 2005

·   Typeset by Artastic Images
Printed in China by Everbest Printing Co. Ltd

National Library of Australia Cataloguing-in-Publication data:

Rothwell, Jo, 1962-.
My Melbourne Adventure.

ISBN 0 9757230 0 6.

1. Melbourne (Vic.) – Juvenile fiction. I. Rothwell, Bryce, 1966-. II. Title.

A823.4

My Melbourne Adventure

Jo Rothwell
Illustrated by
Bryce Rothwell

Rothwell
Publishing

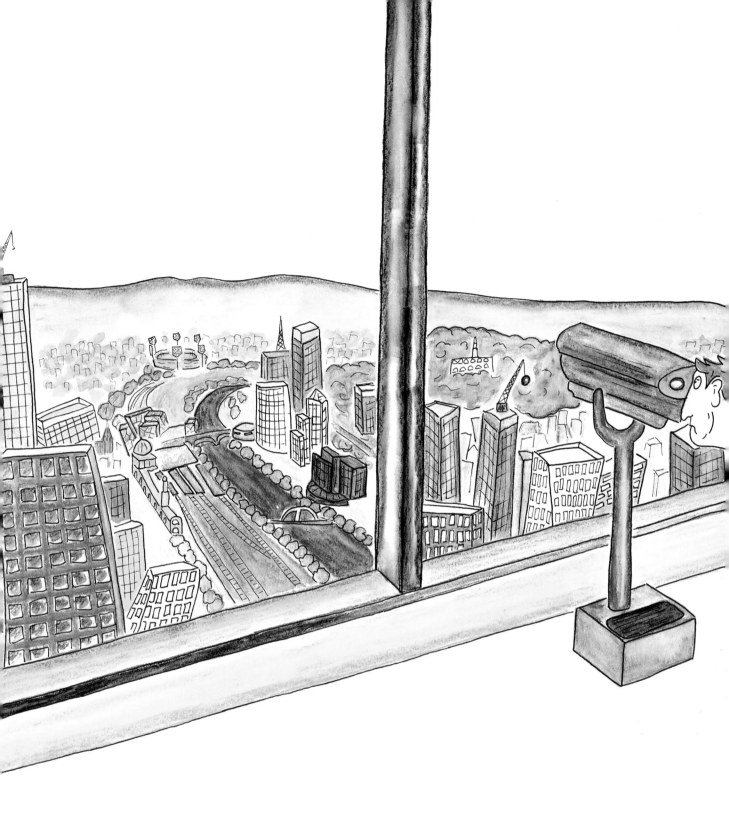

Dear Mac and Pa,
I hope you are well.
I am writing to you with so much to tell.
This is what happened to Nelly and me,
To Melbourne we went......read on and you'll see.

Our adventure began at the Flinders Street Clocks,
We were there to meet Patrick and Hamish, Sally and Scott.

They were coming from their farm and were travelling by train,
But we couldn't find them anywhere........and it had started to rain!

Daddy said perhaps on a tram we would meet,
So we jumped on a tram going up Swanston Street.

We met lots of people who were all very nice,
But our friends were not there........and the rain turned to ice!

We went to the Zoo and the sun then came out.
We couldn't see our friends so I started to shout.
"Patrick and Hamish...where are you?" I say,
"Please come and join our adventure today."

We saw koalas and tigers, kangaroos and bears,
But no Patrick or Hamish; they just were not there.

I thought the Aquarium was where they would be,
Looking at wonders of life in the sea.
There were stingrays, turtles and octopus to view,
Nelly hid from the sharks.......and Daddy did too.

But our friends were not there, what a shame, what a pity,
So where next would we go to explore in this city?

Daddy said perhaps they had gone on to visit,
The Melbourne Museum with its amazing exhibits.

We saw dinosaurs, bugs and old stuff galore,
But we couldn't find our friends...and my feet were getting sore!

Mummy then had a brilliant idea,
We would go to the footy and sit back and cheer.

She said that is where they would certainly be,
So we headed down the road to the MCG.

I was very excited to join in the crowd,
"Go Blues! Go Blues!" I shouted out loud.

And the Magpies said it just wasn't fair,
To lose by one point was too much to bear.

Well Mac and Pa you would have realised I'm sure,
Our friends missed the game and it was raining once more.

So we raced through the gardens to find some sort of shelter,
But the sun shone again and we started to swelter.
These gardens are Royal, majestic and grand.
And Nelly wanted to stay and dig holes in the land.

We then blew past the Shrine and thought of the past,
As a rainbow appeared......but vanished just as fast.

Our friends were **not** in the Gardens **nor** at the Shrine,
So I thought it was best to follow a sign.

Luckily for me the next sign was to go.....
To Luna Park with exciting rides and side shows

We ran through the mouth and were eager to see,
The roller coaster waiting for Mummy and me.

We had a great time on the rides at the fair,
But again we could not find them...our friends were not there.

We went past the Gallery and I got wet from the wall,
And we danced to the music drifting from the Concert Hall.

We then walked about Southbank looking for tea,
And gazed at the Yarra flowing out to the sea.

We had been everywhere;
we had toured the whole city,
And we still could not find them,
indeed what a pity.

So it was time to go back to the Flinders Street Clocks,
And who did we see......Patrick and Hamish, Sally and Scott!

We were astonished to see our friends come into view,
They had only just arrived and said, **"Great to be seeing you"**.
Daddy looked confused and checked the note that had torn,
It read, **"Train Arriving 8 at NIGHT"**......*NOT* 8 in the morn!

We went home to bed to prepare for the next day,
Because our friends were excited about their Melbourne holiday.

They had made a long list of what they wanted to do......
And if you re-read this letter, you'll discover those places too.

Our Melbourne adventure
had come to an end,
And so is this letter I'll
soon have to send,
I know we'll return,
we will often come back,
And you can come too,
Pa and Mac.

Love Always,
Harry XXX

Melbourne Observation Deck

This is at the Rialto Towers and is 253 metres tall. You can see the whole city, you can even see Mount Dandenong. Glad we took the elevator because this only took about 40 seconds to get to the top. Daddy said that the 1254 stairs would be easy to climb. This made Mummy laugh.

Federation Square

This opened in 2002 and is really big and there are so many things there that it would take too long to tell you. So Mac & Pa I think you should just go there yourselves.

Melbourne Zoo

Mac and Pa, this is Australia's oldest zoo. It opened in Parkville in 1862. Fortunately however, the 350 species of animals that are kept there are not that old or they would be pretty slow and tired. These animals are from Australia and all over the world. I really like the elephants....

Carlton Football Club

Formed in 1864....and according to me is the best team in the AFL. There is nothing I need to tell you about Carlton though Pa as you are a very proud and deserving life member.

Collingwood Football Club

Major rivals of Carlton and every other AFL club. Mummy said that my great grandfather followed Collingwood and also Uncle Rob and Aunty Barb. Lucky you were a rebel Pa!

Luna Park

Fantastic fun park in St Kilda. I think however Pa, you should wait to have that milk shake until after you have been on the roller coaster.

Flinders Street Station

This would have to be one of the best places to visit because it's full of trains! Mummy said that they finished building this station in 1910. Wow!

State Library of Victoria

Mummy thinks this is a great place and says that you should take a look at the domed reading room. She says that it is the oldest free public library in Australia and when it opened in 1856 they had 3846 books. Now they have over 2 million. I think it's a great place because they have a copy of this book! Smart people those librarians.

Melbourne Museum

This is a great place full of old stuff like dinosaurs and nature stuff like a rainforest. It even has a section for kiddies like me. You can stand on a scale to see how many wombats you weigh. Mummy didn't want to get on this because she said it wouldn't be fair to the wombats. Nelly agreed.

Royal Botanical Gardens

Great gardens and one of Daddy's favourite places. He started telling us the Latin names of some of the 51,000 plants growing here. That was when Mummy and Nelly and me decided we needed to find the children's garden. Daddy said that these gardens were established in 1846 and is where the National Herbarium of Victoria is. I'm sure this is a good thing.

Arts

Lots of places to go and see arts and hear music and watch plays. But you knew that didn't you!

Melbourne Tram

In my opinion, having a ride on a tram is fantastic. It seems that people get on and off when they need to go to different places. I really don't care where I go, as long as I get there on a tram. There are new trams and old trams... I really like the old ones.

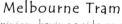

Melbourne Aquarium

This is a fantastic place because you get to see lots of fish and sea creatures and you can even touch some of them. I think that the sea dragons are just amazing because they look like seaweed but are not seaweed but really dragons. I have drawn you a picture of a sea dragon Mac and Pa but I think it looks like seaweed.

Melbourne Cricket Ground (MCG)

This stadium is also for Aussie Rules Football and hosted the 1956 Olympic Games and 2006 Commonwealth Games. Mummy said that she was there in 1970 when Carlton beat Collingwood in the Grand Final. There were 121,696 people there. This is the highest ever football attendance.

Shrine of Remembrance

Daddy said this is a memorial to the people who served Australia in wars. You can leave a poppy.

Yarra River

You can row on it, take a cruise on it, run or ride a bike beside it...and even ski on it. It flows out to Port Phillip Bay and also flows through my beautiful home town of **Warburton**. One of my favourite things to do is to walk our dogs along the Yarra river track.